Seven Little Bunnies

Seven Little Bunnies

by **Julie Stiegemeyer**

pictures by **Laura J. Bryant**

SCHOLASTIC INC.

ISBN 978-1-338-08747-5

Text copyright © 2010 by Julie Stiegemeyer. Illustrations copyright © 2010 by Laura J. Bryant.
Published in the United States by Amazon Publishing, 2010.
This edition made possible under a license arrangement originating with Amazon Publishing, www.apub.com.
All rights reserved. Published by Scholastic Inc., 557 Broadway, New York, NY 10012,
by arrangement with Amazon Children's Publishing. SCHOLASTIC and associated logos are trademarks and/or registered trademarks of Scholastic Inc.

12 11 10 9 8 7 6 5 4 3 2 1   16 17 18 19 20 21

Printed in the U.S.A.   40

First Scholastic printing, April 2016

The illustrations are rendered in watercolor on Strathmore paper.
Book design by Anahid Hamparian
Editor: Margery Cuyler

To Todd and Kathryn
and your little bunnies
—J. S.

To Bun Bun
—L. J. B.

The stars shine in the fading light,
and bunnies soon will say good night.
Mama says, "Climb in your beds,
time to rest your sleepy heads."

Papa says, "Now get some sleep.
I do not want to hear a peep!"
Giggling bunnies hop away.
Seven bunnies want to play.

First little bunny thumps a big drum,
hums and drums with a rum, pum, pum.
Humming, drumming, will he stop?

Cozy,

dozy,

drowsy...

drop.

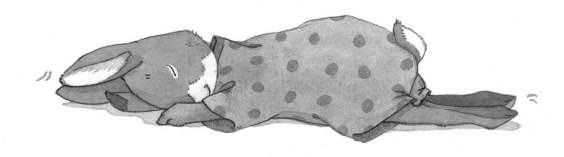

Second little bunny, with a twisting twirl,
dances, leaps with a spinning swirl.
Twirling, swirling, will she stop?

Cozy,

dozy,

drowsy...

drop.

Third little bunny on tiptoe-feet,
searches, spies a bedtime treat.
Munching, crunching, will he stop?

Cozy,

dozy,

drowsy...

drop.

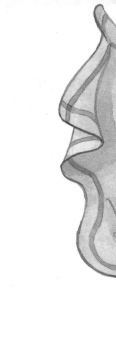

Fourth little bunny with a sneezy nose
sniffs and snuffles, trying to doze.
Sniffling, sneezing, will she stop?

Cozy,

dozy,

drowsy...

drop.

Fifth little bunny with a splash in the tub,
dips and dives with a scrub-a-dub-dub.
Dipping, diving, will he stop?

Cozy,

dozy,

drowsy...

drop.

Sixth little bunny plays basketball,
dribbles, bounces down the hall.
Bouncing, jumping, will she stop?

Cozy,

dozy,

drowsy...

drop.

Seventh little bunny beside the light,
finds a book to read tonight.
Reading, giggling, will he stop?

Cozy,

dozy,

drowsy...

drop.

Seven little bunnies are snug in bed,
with Mama's kiss upon each head.

Then Papa sings a lullaby
about the moon and starry sky.

"When the moon begins to rise,
then it's time to close your eyes.
Stars are twinkling, night is deep.
Now, my bunnies, go to sleep."